Persuading
MISS DOOVER

by Robin Pulver

illustrated by
Stephanie Roth Sisson

Holiday House • New York

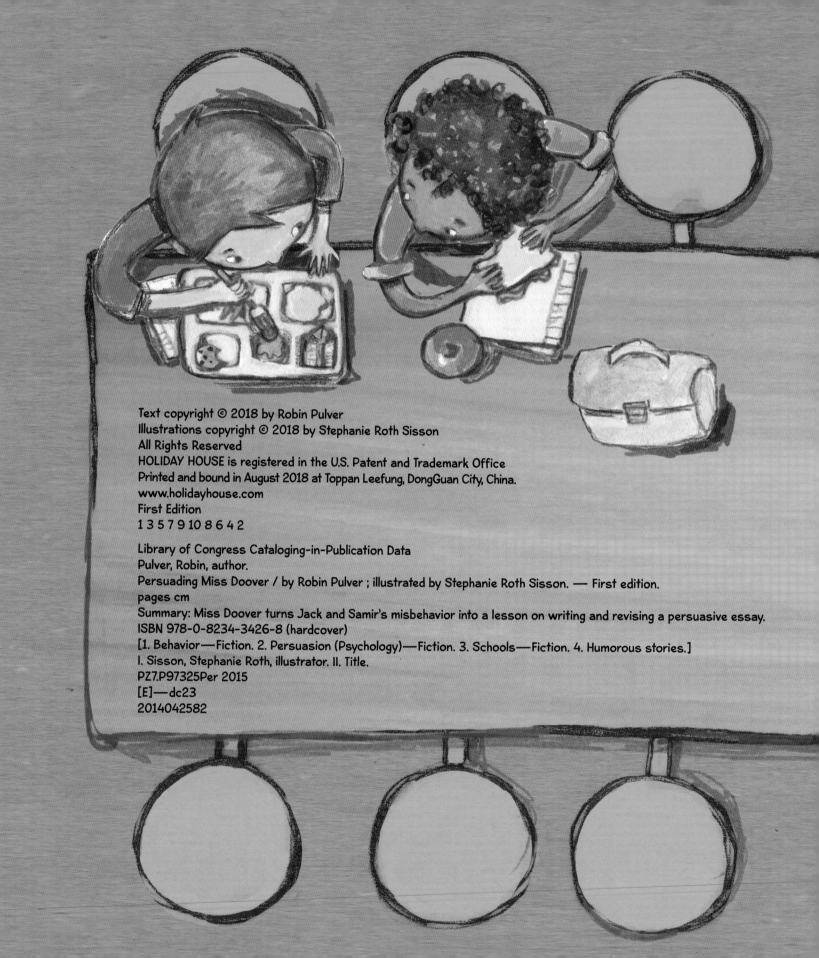

Text copyright © 2018 by Robin Pulver
Illustrations copyright © 2018 by Stephanie Roth Sisson
All Rights Reserved
HOLIDAY HOUSE is registered in the U.S. Patent and Trademark Office
Printed and bound in August 2018 at Toppan Leefung, DongGuan City, China.
www.holidayhouse.com
First Edition
1 3 5 7 9 10 8 6 4 2

Library of Congress Cataloging-in-Publication Data
Pulver, Robin, author.
Persuading Miss Doover / by Robin Pulver ; illustrated by Stephanie Roth Sisson. — First edition.
pages cm
Summary: Miss Doover turns Jack and Samir's misbehavior into a lesson on writing and revising a persuasive essay.
ISBN 978-0-8234-3426-8 (hardcover)
[1. Behavior—Fiction. 2. Persuasion (Psychology)—Fiction. 3. Schools—Fiction. 4. Humorous stories.]
I. Sisson, Stephanie Roth, illustrator. II. Title.
PZ7.P97325Per 2015
[E]—dc23
2014042582

This is for Owen Perkins
(who understands and explains
"Miss Doover" so well) and for
my persuasive grand nephews,
Ouju, Harry, and Cooper.
—R. P.

To Robin Pulver
—S. R. S.

Just then the principal, Mr. Humphry, came in.

Harrumph! I have a difficult announcement to make. Harrumph!

I'm sorry, but the field trip to the farm has been canceled. There's no money for it in the budget.

Harrumph! I enjoy jokes as well as the next guy, but this is no laughing matter. Harrumph! Let's see what's so funny.

Mr. Humphry stomped out of the room.

Miss Doover sank into her chair, her head in her hands.

Miss Doover sat Jack in the front of the room.
She sent Samir to a seat in the back.

The next morning, Jack put a shiny apple on Miss Doover's desk.

Me and Samir should sit together. School's no fun if we can't. We could conspire to learn better. It's mean to separate best friends.

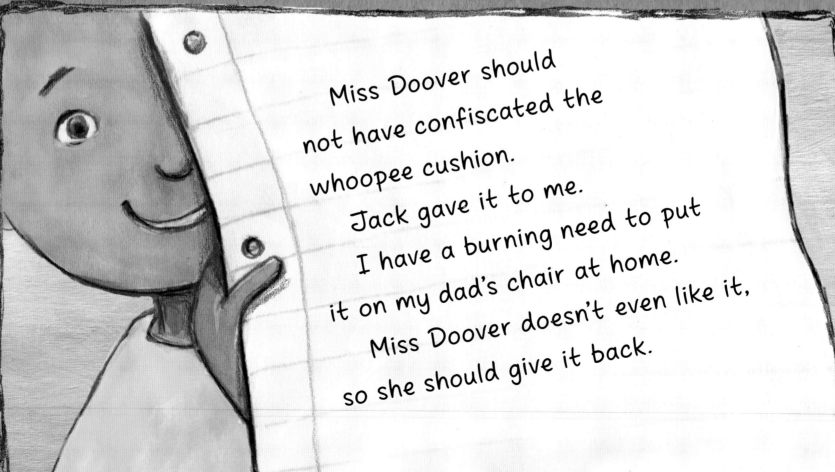

Miss Doover should
not have confiscated the
whoopee cushion.
Jack gave it to me.
I have a burning need to put
it on my dad's chair at home.
Miss Doover doesn't even like it,
so she should give it back.

My dog should be our class pet.
She has soft, thick hair.
Petting a dog is good for your health.
Miss Doover wouldn't get so stressed about tests if she could pet my dog at school.

We should be allowed to take more than two books out of the library at a time.
I'm a fast reader.
I finish two books the first day I take them out.
I'll learn more if I can take out more than two books at a time.

We learn best when we're having fun.

Two-hour recess would be educational.

Recess should be for two hours. We would have more time for fun and frivolity.

Miss Doover should give Samir and me another chance to sit together. Then we won't have to yell across the room to talk to each other. WE PROMISE TO BE GOOD!!!!! (That is true. It is not hyperbole.) Miss Doover's life will be happier if we don't have to bug her about sitting together.